## Zachary Archer Cohn

Zachary was a sweet, smart, and curious boy who adored his family. He has a big sister, Jenna, a little brother, Henry, a little sister, Sydney, and a Mom and Dad who miss him every day.

Zachary loved superheroes, wearing shorts and flip-flops year round, and learning how things worked. He especially treasured his stuffed polar bear.

One of Zachary's favorite places to be was in the water. He loved to jump and splash, and would spend hours with his goggles on, exploring underwater.

In 2007, Zachary passed away in a drain entrapment in a backyard pool. The ZAC Foundation was created in his memory to teach water safety skills and serve as a resource for making pools safer. The Foundation is dedicated to ending childhood drownings nationwide.

Since its inception, the Foundation has launched ZAC Camps, which teach children the ABC and Ds of water safety through swimming lessons, safety classes with First Responders, and classroom instruction. To learn more about The ZAC Foundation, visit www.thezacfoundation.com.

This book is forever dedicated in Zachary's loving memory.

# The Polar Bear
# Who Couldn't, Wouldn't Swim

## By Karen and Brian Cohn
### Illustrated by Brent Beck

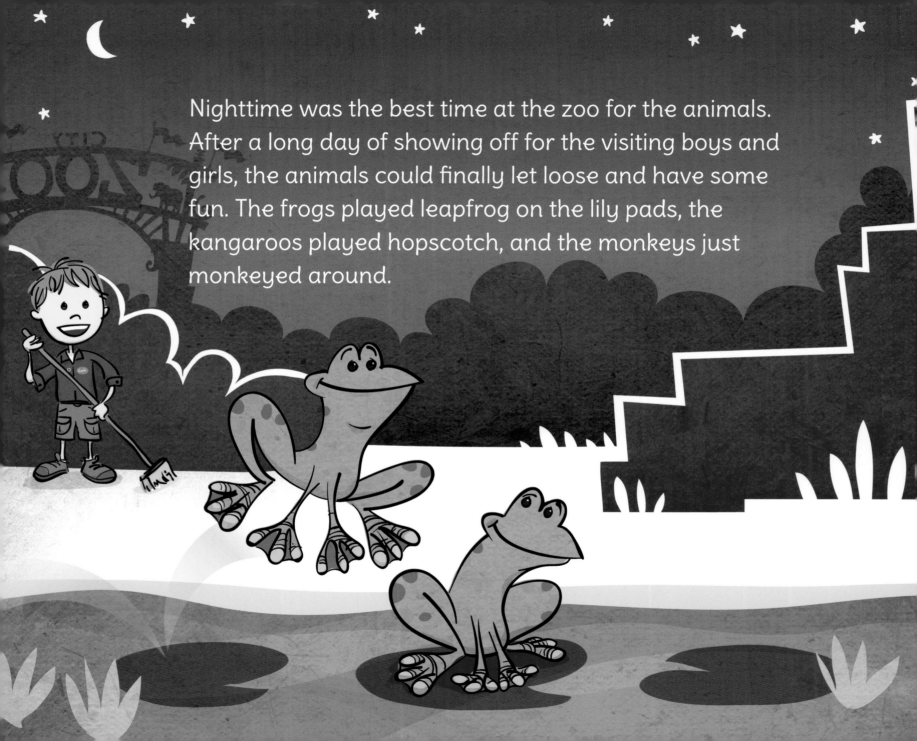

Nighttime was the best time at the zoo for the animals. After a long day of showing off for the visiting boys and girls, the animals could finally let loose and have some fun. The frogs played leapfrog on the lily pads, the kangaroos played hopscotch, and the monkeys just monkeyed around.

Across the zoo, the polar bear family shared in the fun. Three young cubs, Jenna, Henry, and Sydney splashed in their pool while their mom watched. Just like most polar bears, the cubs loved to swim.

But not their brother, Zeke. He never joined in the fun. He was afraid of the water and sat by himself bouncing his favorite ball, hoping to be left alone.

He just couldn't and wouldn't swim.

But on this night, Zeke lost control of his ball and it started to roll toward the pool! "Oh no!" Zeke shouted as he scrambled to his paws and sprinted after the ball. He couldn't let the ball fall into the water, and as he ran he could hear his mom yelling, "Don't run by the pool!" But he did not listen.

Zeke was close to grabbing the ball, but when he lunged for it, his paw slipped and he tumbled into the water.

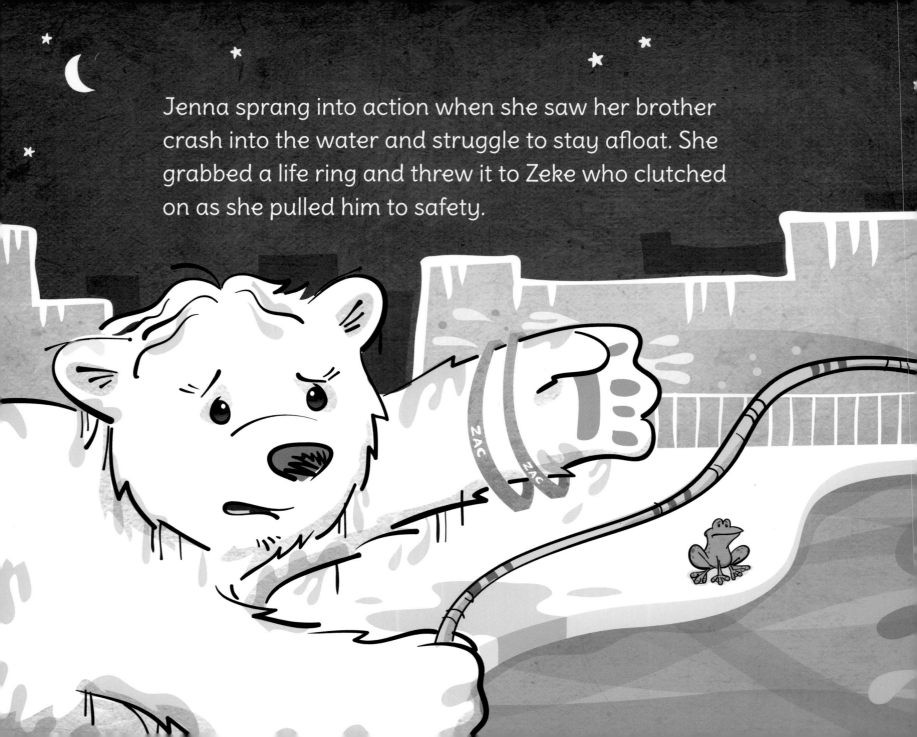

Jenna sprang into action when she saw her brother crash into the water and struggle to stay afloat. She grabbed a life ring and threw it to Zeke who clutched on as she pulled him to safety.

Zeke shivered with embarrassment, wondering what his family thought about a polar bear who couldn't and wouldn't swim. He knew he had to go somewhere animals couldn't and wouldn't swim, too. But where?

Just then, Zeke thought of his friend, Parker the Penguin. He looked around at his family enjoying the water and made his choice. Zeke sneaked off to see Parker.

PENGUINS

POLAR BEARS

"Hiya, Zeke!" shouted Parker when he spotted Zeke in the penguin habitat. "What are you up to?"

"I don't want to live by the water because I can't swim and don't feel safe," explained Zeke. "Penguins don't swim, so I want to live with you."

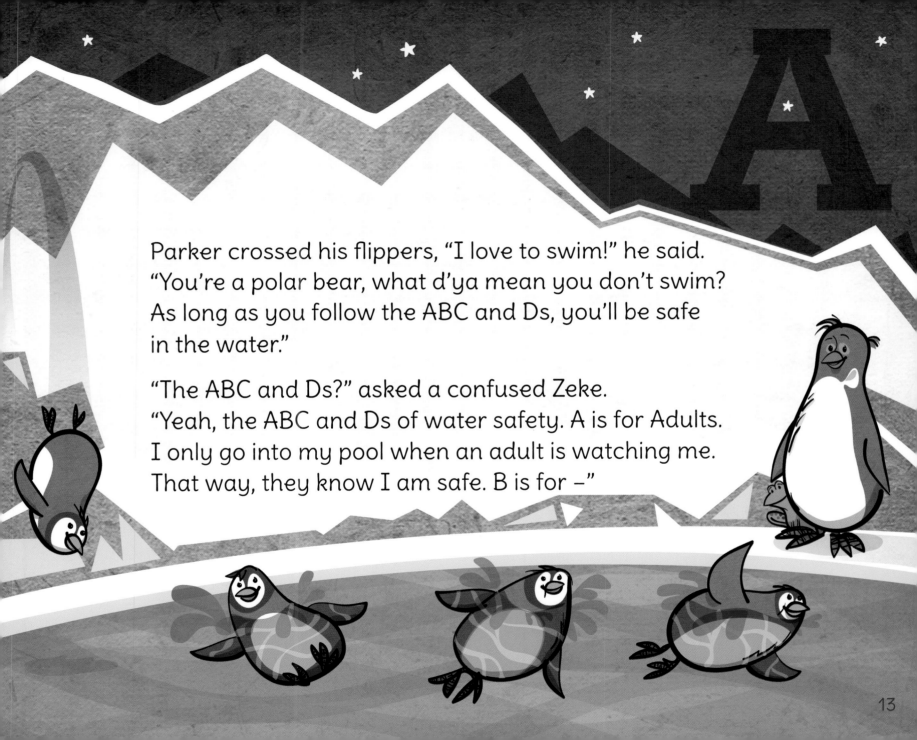

Parker crossed his flippers, "I love to swim!" he said. "You're a polar bear, what d'ya mean you don't swim? As long as you follow the ABC and Ds, you'll be safe in the water."

"The ABC and Ds?" asked a confused Zeke. "Yeah, the ABC and Ds of water safety. A is for Adults. I only go into my pool when an adult is watching me. That way, they know I am safe. B is for –"

"No, no, no," Zeke interrupted. "Maybe you like the water, but it is too scary for me." Zeke turned around, not wanting to hear any more, and left.

He couldn't and wouldn't swim.

*Now where should I go?* Zeke thought to himself. "Ah ha!" he said aloud. There was no way the largest animals in the zoo could swim. They were just too big! Zeke sprinted off to see his friend, Elliot the Elephant.

As soon as Zeke got to the elephant habitat, he saw Elliot splashing his dad in the pool.

"Hey, Zeke. Come on in!" shouted Elliot.

Zeke couldn't believe his eyes. "I didn't know you could swim," Zeke sighed.

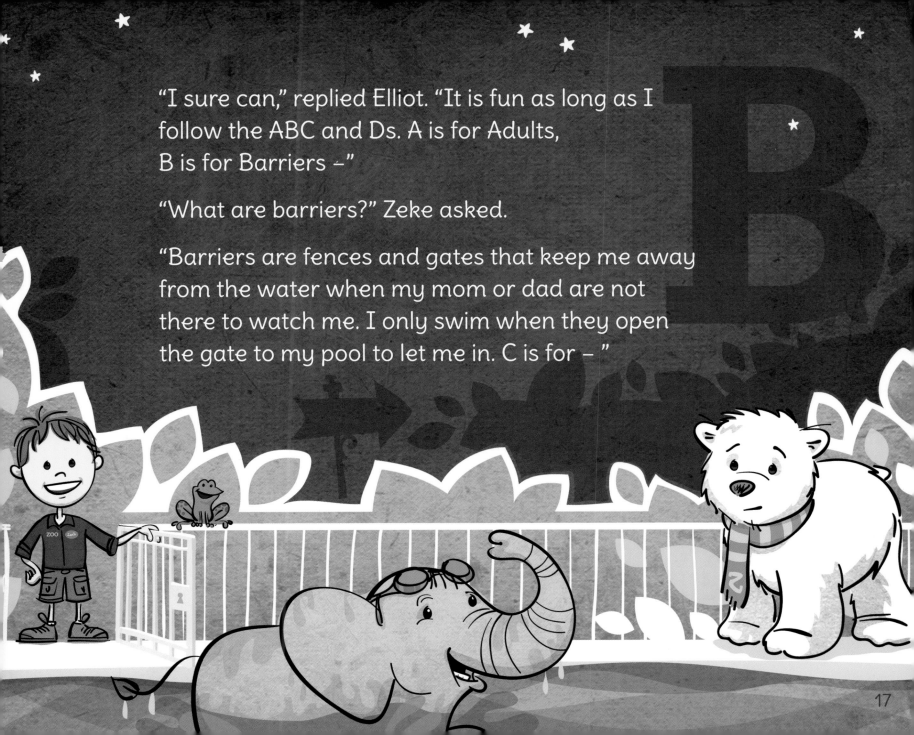

"I sure can," replied Elliot. "It is fun as long as I follow the ABC and Ds. A is for Adults, B is for Barriers –"

"What are barriers?" Zeke asked.

"Barriers are fences and gates that keep me away from the water when my mom or dad are not there to watch me. I only swim when they open the gate to my pool to let me in. C is for – "

17

Before Elliot could finish, Zeke stood up shaking his head. He did not want to hear about how swimming could be safe or fun.

He couldn't and wouldn't swim.

He said a quick goodbye to Elliot, and Elliot just shrugged and waved his trunk. Zeke was confused and sad. Could he be the only animal in the zoo afraid of the water? Everyone loved the water – penguins, polar bears, and even elephants!

But Zeke couldn't swim. He wouldn't swim. And he knew he had to keep going. He wondered what animal he could live with who wouldn't swim. Finally, he had his answer and he hurried off to see Hanna the Hippo.

When he arrived, Hanna was prancing around the hippo pool practicing her ballet as her mom watched nearby. Zeke was happy to see his friend not swimming, but his hopes washed away when Hanna broke her stride and launched into a giant cannonball right into the pool.

Hanna came up laughing, "I totally got you!" Zeke stood there, shivering and soaked. "Oh, I'm sorry, Zeke," said Hanna. "I only wanted to surprise you."

"It's not you," he said, "I'm scared of swimming. I want to live somewhere without water, but everyone swims."

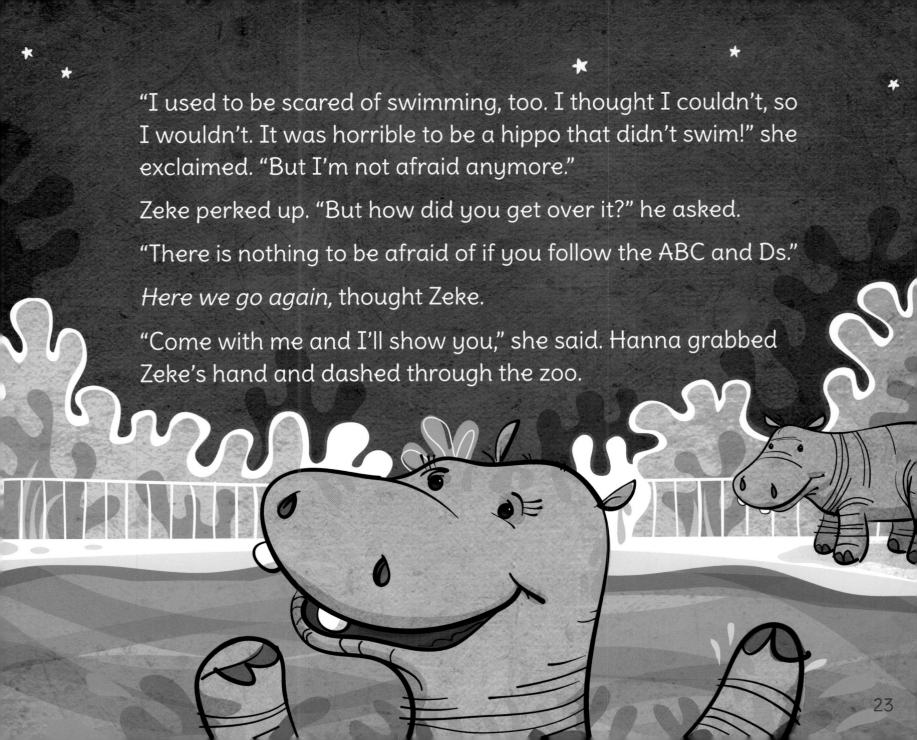

"I used to be scared of swimming, too. I thought I couldn't, so I wouldn't. It was horrible to be a hippo that didn't swim!" she exclaimed. "But I'm not afraid anymore."

Zeke perked up. "But how did you get over it?" he asked.

"There is nothing to be afraid of if you follow the ABC and Ds."

*Here we go again*, thought Zeke.

"Come with me and I'll show you," she said. Hanna grabbed Zeke's hand and dashed through the zoo.

23

When they finally stopped running, Zeke was terrified to see the biggest and scariest pool he had ever seen.

"Wh-where are we?" he stuttered.

"Let's sit down," Hanna replied.

Zeke trusted his friend, so they sat together at the edge of the pool.

Just then, a lone, dark fin popped out of the water and started to speed toward Zeke and Hanna. Zeke tried and tried to get his friend to stand up, but she wouldn't budge. The dark fin was getting too close!

Zeke prepared for the worst.

"Daisy!" shouted Hanna. Zeke opened one eye, then the other. There in front of him was Daisy the Dolphin.

"Hi, Hanna. Who's your friend?" asked Daisy.

"This is Zeke. He is afraid to get in the pool," Hanna said.

"Do you remember the A and B of safety? C is for Classes," Hanna explained to Zeke. "After taking classes with Daisy, I knew how to swim and be safe around water. She can teach you, too!"

Daisy looked at Zeke, "It's true. I could teach you to swim. It's easy. Come on in." Daisy extended her fins and Zeke looked into the deep blue water not sure what to do. He could walk away and go home right now, or he could face his fear tonight.

He stared down at the water and thought about what to do. No more sitting alone, no more couldn'ts, no more wouldn'ts, and no more being the only polar bear who was afraid to swim.

Trusting in Daisy, Zeke jumped into her fins and held his breath. He was surprised when Daisy caught him before he went under. She held him up and he felt safe in the water for the first time.

They spent all night in the water learning how to swim. And before the swimming lesson was over, Daisy said, "Don't forget about the D of the ABC and Ds! D is for Drains. Make sure you always stay away from pool drains because you can become stuck to them. Most animals don't know about the D, but now you do!"

Knowing the ABC and Ds of water safety helped Zeke learn to swim. He promised Daisy he would come back to swim with her. It was fun! When it was time to go home, Zeke said the ABC and Ds one more time so he wouldn't forget:

**A** is for Adult,

**B** is for Barriers,

**C** is for Classes, and

**D** is for Drains.

By the time the sun came up, Zeke was back with his family, snuggling with Jenna, Henry, and Sydney. When he woke, the zoo had opened and kids were lining up to catch a glimpse of the great polar bears.

Zeke proudly stood up and walked toward the pool.

After his mom opened the gate, Zeke checked to make sure she was watching. He remembered his classes from the night before, and he jumped in.

When he came up, all the kids were clapping loudly, excited to see the young polar bear playing in the water.

From that day on, whenever animals in the zoo were afraid of the water, Zeke taught them how to be safe with the ABC and Ds and brought them to see Daisy for her special swimming lessons. Never again did a young animal say he couldn't and wouldn't, because Zeke was there to show them they could and they should.

# THE END

# The ABC and Ds of Water Safety

Now that Zeke knows the ABC and Ds, he wants you to be safe in the water, too!
Make sure you remember the ABC and Ds of Water Safety before you go in the water.

## A is for Adult:

- Always have an adult with you around water.
- Never be alone near a pool, ocean, lake, or river.
- Adults must always have their eyes on you in the water.
  If you can't see an adult's eyes, they can't see you!

## B is for Barrier:

- Respect barriers, such as a fence that goes around a pool, to keep you
  safe from dangers in the water.
- Do not enter the pool area until an adult has opened the pool gate.
- Never climb over a pool fence or gate to get to the water.